Grannie's

The Mainland

The New Pier

The Jetty

TO THE NEW PIER

CRAFTS

ISLE of STRUAY SHOP & POST OFFICE

OBAN TIMES
GET YOUR COPY HERE

BISTRO

WELCOME

WEST HIGHLAND FREE PRESS
ORDER NOW

The Shop & Post Office

The
Katie Morag
Treasury

The Katie Morag Treasury

THE BODLEY HEAD
LONDON

Contents

A Letter to Katie Morag
6

Katie Morag's Family Tree
8

The Isle of Struay
10

Katie Morag's Room
12

Katie Morag Delivers the Mail
15

Granpa's Bowl – *from Grannie Island's Ceilidh*
41

Katie Morag and the Two Grandmothers
49

The Big Smelly Goat – *from Grannie Island's Ceilidh*
75

Katie Morag and the Tiresome Ted
83

Hugh Handy – *from Grannie Island's Ceilidh*
109

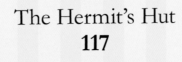

The Hermit's Hut
117

The Gardens of Struay
124

Castle McColl
129

Footprints on the Beach
140

Stone Soup – *from Grannie Island's Ceilidh*
143

Katie Morag and the Dancing Class
151

Annie Jessie and the Merboy – *from Grannie Island's Ceilidh*
177

Katie Morag and the Big Boy Cousins
185

Little Izzy – *from Grannie Island's Ceilidh*
211

The Isle of Struay Map
218

Windy Weather
220

The Katie Morag Quiz
222

A Letter to Katie Morag

Dear Katie Morag,

What does it feel like to see yourself in a book? When I thought you up in my head, many, many years ago, I never believed you would end up in so many books and become so famous. And now you are on TV!

You were just the little girl I always wanted to be; a girl who had red hair and lived on a little island and had endless adventures that I could write stories about. I loved drawing you and your family and friends.

I so enjoyed illustrating all the pictures of your island with its Village, the boats and beaches, its animals and birds. And especially Grannie Island's dog, her tractor and her favourite sheep, Alecina. I used to have a sheep called Alecina. You didn't know that, did you?

There are many people who try to find your island, the Isle of Struay, but we will keep that a secret, won't we? Ssh! Don't tell anyone – we made the name up, didn't we?

Now it is time to let everyone explore your island for themselves. It is good to know that you are there to lead them on, Clan Chief Katie Morag McColl!

Lots of Love,

Mairi Hedderwick

P.S. I've enjoyed writing to you, Katie Morag. 'East West, Letter's Best', as Grannie Island would say.

7

KATIE MORAG'S FAMILY TREE

Gertrude Isobel Tilsley (Bel)
(Historian & Crofter)

M.

Capt. Nils J. Olsen
(Helicopter pilot)

GRANNIE ISLAND

Sven & Sean Olsen (TWINS)
(Singer & Cellist)

Isobel Olsen
(Postmistress)

M.

Peter McColl
(Shopkeeper)

Katie Morag McColl

Liam McColl

Flora Ann McColl

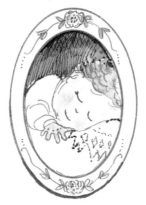

KATIE MORAG

8

Grace Margaret Nicol (Meg)
(Retired Nurse & Secretary)

M. Hector Archibald McColl (1)
(Butcher – deceased)

Neilly Beag (2)
(Crofter)

GRANMA
MAINLAND

James McColl M. Rachel Stoddart
(Reverend)

Matthew McColl

Hector McColl   Archie McColl   Dougal McColl   Jamie McColl   Murdo Iain McColl

THE BIG BOY COUSINS

THE ISLE of STRUAY

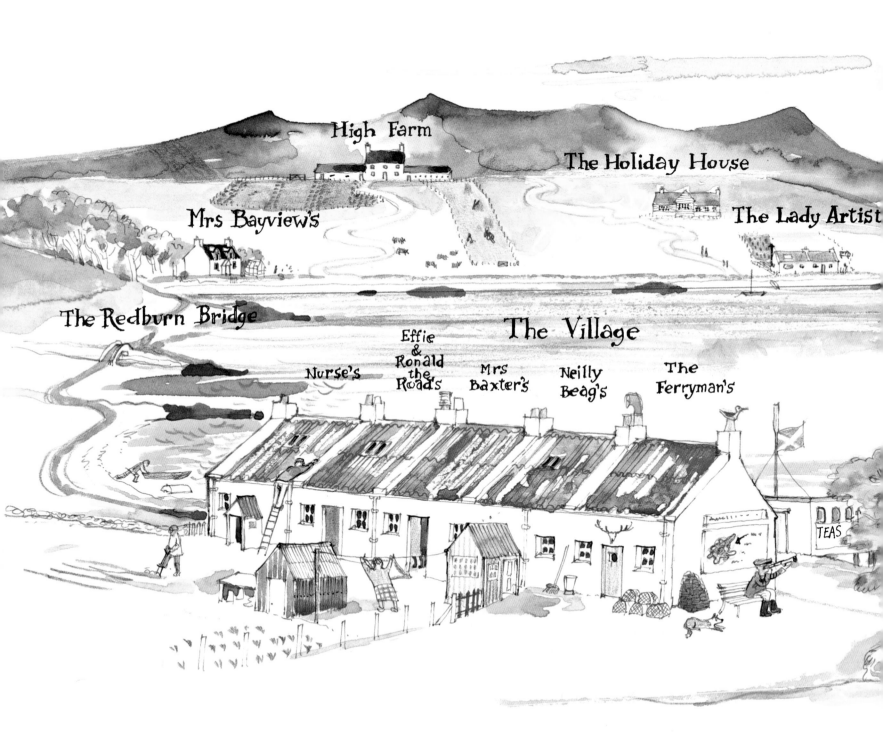

High Farm

The Holiday House

Mrs Bayview's

The Lady Artist

The Redburn Bridge

The Village

Nurse's

Effie
&
Ronald
the
Road's

Mrs
Baxter's

Neilly
Beag's

The
Ferryman's

TEAS

Grannie's

The Mainland

The New Pier

The Jetty

CRAFTS

TO THE
NEW PIER

ISLE of STRUAY
SHOP & POST OFFICE

OBAN
TIMES

GET
YOUR COPY
HERE

BISTRO

WELCOME

WEST
HIGHLAND
FREE PRESS

ORDER
NOW

The Shop & Post Office

11

Katie Morag's Room

When Katie Morag is in a good mood, her bedroom looks like this:

When Katie Morag is in a bad mood, THIS is what her bedroom looks like: "This room is a MIDDEN!" shrieks Mrs McColl.

To all small places

Katie Morag
Delivers the Mail

Wednesdays were always hectic on the Isle of Struay, for that was the day that the boat brought mail and provisions from the mainland.

One particular Wednesday was worse than usual, since baby Liam was cutting his first tooth and both Mr and Mrs McColl were in a bad mood.

"All right, all right," said Mrs McColl in exasperation. "I'll take Liam upstairs to quieten him down! Katie Morag, you take the mail to the houses across the Bay. There are five parcels – one for each house. The one with the red label is for Grannie."

Pleased to escape, Katie Morag set off. She loved any excuse to visit her Grannie, who lived all alone in the very last house on the other side of the Bay.

But it was a hot day, and Katie Morag had just stopped for a moment to paddle in a pool beneath the Redburn Bridge, when suddenly – *splash!* – she slipped on a slithery stone and fell into the water, mailbag and all.

"Oh, dear! Oh, dear!" wailed Katie Morag looking at the five soggy parcels.
"All the addresses are smudged and I won't know which parcel is for which house now!"
Only Grannie's parcel was still recognizable by its red label.

Then, because she was so frightened and ashamed, Katie Morag did a silly thing. She ran the rest of the way to the other side of the Bay and threw a parcel – any parcel, except the red-labelled one – on to the doorstep of each of the first four houses.

Nobody saw her. Still sobbing, she ran on to Grannie's.

"Well, this is a fine *boorach* you've got yourself into, Katie Morag," said Grannie, when Katie Morag had explained what she had done. "Still at least you've given *me* the right parcel – it's got the spare part for the tractor that I've been waiting for. I'll go and get the old grey lady going, while you dry yourself up. Then you can try and sort the whole muddle out."

Grannie had her head under the bonnet of the tractor for a long time.
Occasionally, Katie Morag heard muffled words of anger and she thought
of the angry words waiting for her at home . . .

Then, suddenly, with a cough of black smoke, the tractor stuttered into
life and they set off to go round each of the four houses in turn.

The first house belonged to the Lady Artist. She had been expecting tiny, thin brushes for her miniature paintings, but the parcel Katie Morag had left on her doorstep contained two enormous brushes.

"They're bigger than my painting boards!" she said in disgust.

The second house was rented by the Holiday People. They had ordered
fishing hooks from a sports catalogue, but their parcel had been full of garden seeds.
"We can't fish with daisies and lettuces!" they complained.

At the third house, Mr MacMaster was standing by a big barrel of whitewash, holding the Lady Artist's paint brushes.

"How can I paint my walls with these fiddling little things?" he asked.

In the fourth house lived Mrs Bayview. "That stupid shop on the mainland! Where are my seeds? Flowers won't grow out of *these*," she said crossly, waving a packet of fishing hooks in the air.

After much trundling back and forth, Katie Morag finally managed
to collect and deliver all the right things to all the right people.
Everyone smiled and waved and said, "Thank you very much."

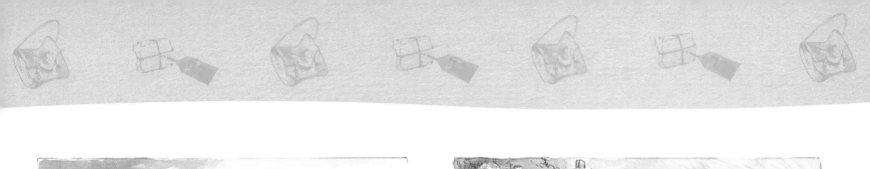

By now it was getting dark. Katie Morag thought of the long journey home. She would be very late and her parents were so bad-tempered these days on account of Liam's noisy teething.

"Grannie, would you like to come back for tea?" she asked.

Katie Morag half hid behind Grannie as they walked in the kitchen door but,
to her surprise, everyone was smiling. Liam had cut his tooth at last and all was calm.

"Thank you for helping out today, Katie Morag," said Mrs McColl. "Isn't she good, Grannie?"

"Och aye," said Grannie with a smile as she looked at Katie Morag. "She's very good at sorting things out, is our Katie Morag." And she said no more.

Granpa's Bowl

A folk tale told at Grannie Island's Ceilidh by Mr McColl

This is a story about a woman called Mrs Finlayson, who lived in a wee croft near the Deserted Village, not too long ago. She lived with her husband and her two children, Donald, who was eight, and Maggie, nearly six. The family were poor, but Mrs Finlayson always made sure the children were fed and clothed, and anyone who knew her would say what a kind and helpful friend she was. But despite her many good points, Mrs Finlayson was not happy; she would get very grumpy sometimes, and her face would go all tight and twisted, like she was eating a lemon, but forgot to add sugar. The family would try not to laugh, but the reason that Mrs Finlayson was grumpy was that she believed she wasn't quite as good as everyone else. She couldn't help but feel ashamed of their little house and how poor they were. And when she felt like that, the lemony face would appear.

Now in those days, a very rich woman would come to Struay every summer for her holidays, and stay in the big Holiday House. One particular day, Mrs Finlayson met the Holiday Woman in the shop. Just as she was leaving, the Ferryman's Wife came in, and to Mrs Finlayson's amazement, the Holiday Woman said, "Marvellous high tea yesterday, Mrs Ferrywoman – delicious cake, thank you."

Well, you could have blown Mrs Finlayson down with a feather! Imagine inviting the Holiday Woman to high tea? The very idea of such a person seeing inside her own poor little cottage filled her with embarrassment.

Yet Mrs Ferryman's cottage was much the same as hers. She didn't know where it came from, but she was as surprised as everyone else when she heard herself saying, "Perhaps you would like to come for lunch next Tuesday?"

The Holiday Woman smiled and said, "Why, I would be delighted!"

The days leading up to the Holiday Woman's visit were a hurly burly of preparation. Mrs Finlayson cleaned the entire cottage from top to bottom. Maggie collected flowers for the table, and Donald had to take a handful of books and place them above the fireplace, just as if they were always there and often read. But still, Mrs Finlayson worried. And the reason was a person I haven't yet mentioned – a very old man by the name of Murdo.

Now Murdo was the children's grandfather; a kind, gentle man, he'd lived with the family since before Maggie was born. But he was now very frail and not steady with his hands, so sometimes at meal times, he'd struggle to feed himself and much of his dinner landed on the table or the floor. Mrs Finlayson was a kindly woman and she rarely complained when Murdo made a mess, but rarely isn't never, so she bought a deep clay bowl for Murdo and it meant the food didn't skitter off so easily. It was known as "Granpa's Bowl" and no one else ever used it.

Tuesday lunch arrived and the Finlayson family dressed in their Sunday Best, opened the door to the Holiday Woman, and welcomed her into their house. At first everything went well: the Holiday Woman made *ooh* and *aah* noises about the "darling little house". She chatted to the children, who were on their best behaviour, and Mrs Finlayson began to relax.

Murdo made a great effort to delicately eat the delicious soup Mrs Finlayson had prepared from the spinach they grew on the croft. It might have been better if he hadn't made quite such an effort. You see, to try and be tidy, he lifted the bowl to his lips, but he lost his grip and it slipped from his fingers! In his panic, Murdo gave the bowl an almighty thwack and it tumbled through the air . . . and exploded in front of the Holiday Woman, showering her with bright green spinach soup!

Everyone looked at the green sludge making its way from her blonde curls, down over her surprised face, to its destination – the front of her pretty pink, casual day jacket.

Suddenly, Mrs Finlayson leapt into action. She snatched up a napkin and started wiping the pink jacket, but all she did was spread the stain further and deeper. The Holiday Woman was kind and gracious, but Mrs Finlayson could tell she was upset. So you can guess what expression Mrs Finlayson made . . . Yep, lemony face!

Poor Murdo felt terrible, and he left the table without saying a word. The Holiday Woman finished her soup, and when it was time to leave politely declared she'd had a delightful time. But as she shut the door, Mrs Finlayson said, "That's it . . . Murdo is only to have bread and butter in his room from now on!" What had she been thinking inviting the Holiday Woman to lunch? She was a penniless nobody, and penniless nobodies should remember their place.

An hour passed, the afternoon was marching to evening, and still feeling cross, she went back to the kitchen – where, to her surprise, she found Maggie and Donald sitting at the table, with the broken pieces of Granpa's Bowl and a small jar of glue.

"What on earth are you doing?" she asked.

"Fixing Granpa's Bowl," Maggie replied.

"I can see that. Why?" asked Mrs Finlayson.

Maggie sighed, "We supposed that Granpa wouldn't need it now – you said he's only allowed bread and butter. But one day you'll be old like him, and we will be too, so we'll need the bowl for when our time comes."

Well, her daughter's wise words broke Mrs Finlayson's heart. She began to cry. She cried until wee Maggie came over and put her arms round her. Then a funny thing happened – she began to laugh, and Maggie laughed, and Donald joined in, and they laughed until tears ran down their cheeks.

Then Mrs Finlayson went to Murdo and told him that she was truly sorry, and that she'd heat a fresh bowl of soup and would be honoured if he'd join her at the table. And that's exactly what he did; that day, and every day that followed.

Of course, he still spilled some from time to time, but a little soup on the tablecloth never hurt anyone. And as for the Holiday Woman, well, she got most of the stain out of her jacket. But on sunny days, Mrs Finlayson was sure she could still see the merest trace of green. In the past this would have filled her with shame, but something had changed in her that day. And the stain on the Holiday Woman's jacket . . . well, it merely made her smile.

To all Grandmothers – Big or Wee

Katie Morag
and the Two Grandmothers

One sunny Wednesday morning Mrs McColl woke Katie Morag early. "Hurry up, now!" she said, drawing back the curtains. "Here comes the boat. Granma Mainland will be here soon and you've still got this room to tidy for her."

Granma Mainland lived far away in the big city. She was coming to stay with them for a holiday.

Katie Morag went with her other grandmother, Grannie Island, who lived just across the Bay, to meet the boat.

"My, you're still a smart wee Bobby Dazzler," said Neilly Beag, as he helped Granma Mainland down.

Grannie Island revved the engine *very* loudly. BUROOM . . . BUROOM . . . BUROOM . . .

Katie Morag watched, fascinated, as Granma Mainland unpacked.

"Do you like this new hat I've brought for Show Day, Katie Morag?" Granma Mainland asked.

"Och, her and her fancy ways!" muttered Grannie Island to herself.

Show Day was always a big event on the Island of Struay. At the Post Office, Mr and Mrs McColl were rushed off their feet.

"*Look* where you're GOING!" shouted Mrs McColl, as Katie Morag tripped over baby Liam.

"Katie Morag, I think you'd be better off helping Grannie Island get Alecina ready for the Show," sighed Mr McColl.

Alecina was Grannie Island's prize sheep. She had won the Best Ewe and Fleece Trophy for the past seven years, but she was getting old, and everyone said that Neilly Beag's April Love would win it this year.

Katie Morag ran as fast as she could, past the Show Field, where frantic last-minute preparations were in progress, and on to Grannie Island's in order to give Alecina an extra special brush and comb before the judging started.

Refreshments

BAYVIEW BARROW

But when Katie Morag arrived at Grannie Island's, Alecina was up to her horns in the Boggy Loch.

"A whole hillside to eat and she wants *that* blade of grass!" cried Grannie Island in a fury.

"Look at your fleece! And today of *all* days, you old devil!" ranted Grannie Island when they eventually got Alecina out of the Boggy Loch. "We'll never get these peaty stains out in time for the Show!"

"Granma Mainland has some stuff to make *her* hair silvery white . . ." said Katie Morag thoughtfully.

Isle of Stru ow

HOME
PRODUCE

HANDICRAFTS

CHILDREN'S SPORTS

LADIES

Pe er

Everyone looked in amazement as Grannie Island's old tractor
and trailer hurtled past the Show Field, heading for the Post Office.
"We'll be too late!" grumbled Grannie Island.

Fortunately, no one was about when they got
home, since Mrs McColl would certainly not
have approved of this . . .

. . . or this.

And Granma Mainland would have been furious at this . . .

. . . not to mention this.

But all ended well. They managed to get tidied up and back to the Show Field just in time for the judging, and, at the sight of Alecina's shiny coat and curls, the judges were in no doubt as to who should win the Silver Trophy again this year.

That evening there was a party at Grannie Island's to celebrate.

"My, but thon old ewe is still some beauty for her age," said Neilly Beag.

"Just like yourself, Granma Mainland. How do you do it?"

"Ah, that's *my* secret," said wee Granma Mainland, fluttering her eyelashes.

Katie Morag and Grannie Island smiled at each other. They knew some of the secret, but would never tell.

And Grannie Island never frowned at Granma Mainland's "fancy ways" ever again. I wonder why?

The Big Smelly Goat

A folk tale told at Grannie Island's Ceilidh by Grannie Island

This story happened a long, long time ago, around Harvest time, when the berries were ripe, and the land was brown from the sun.

Folk lived in the Deserted Village, a friendly place, and they were always ready to lend a hand when a neighbour needed help. One of the people who lived in the Deserted Village was Grannie Island's own great-great-grandmother. In later years, everyone knew her as Grannie Two Teeth, but back then she was just a young woman, so folk called her Morag.

Morag lived with her husband James and two young children in a little house in the middle of the village, and she had a very dear friend, a lady called Nessa Campbell, who lived over by the Heron Road, with her husband, Ruraidh, and eight children: seven sons and one wee baby girl. The Campbells were poor, as most folk were, and their house was very small. Oh, poor Nessa did her best to keep the place clean and tidy, but with all those people living there, it wasn't easy. In fact, it was a midden!

One day Nessa dropped by Morag's house looking miserable. Her boys were growing bigger every day, and as they grew bigger the house seemed to shrink. And the noise – it was more than a person could bear. Morag felt sorry for Nessa, but the only help she could offer was to listen and give her a hot cup of tea.

It so happened that the very next day, a *cailleach*, which is the Gaelic word for a wise woman, was on her way to collect some special plants which grew on the shore. The cailleach always stopped by Morag's for a chat. As they chatted, Morag mentioned Nessa's problem. The cailleach nodded wisely, and asked Morag to take her to Nessa's house. Well, Morag and the cailleach could hear the din from the little house before they could see it. The boys were yelling and running around, and the baby was crying for the fun of it. Yet as bad as the noise was, the mess was even worse! No sooner had Nessa tidied something than three more things were scattered.

Eventually, she just gave up and sat miserably at the kitchen table, which is how Morag and the cailleach found her when they arrived. Nessa put on her best smile and offered them a cup of tea.

Oh, but the cailleach said no! She wasn't there to drink tea, she was there to help. The cailleach looked round, then closed her eyes. And when she opened them again, she nodded, and said the solution was obvious: Nessa needed a goat, a big, smelly goat. Well, Morag frowned. Of all the things Nessa needed, a big smelly goat was not the most obvious. But the cailleach didn't have the slightest doubt. This goat was to live in the house with the family for seven days and seven nights. And that was that.

That same afternoon, the cailleach accompanied Nessa and Morag across the island to the Wild Goat Place, where there was a tiny hut. And the kindly old shepherd loaned Nessa one of his goats. It was a very large and very smelly goat. Not like the Lady Artist's lovely wee thing. It was also the most cantankerous animal Morag had ever met, but this seemed to please the cailleach. And so began the longest week of poor Nessa's life; hard as things had been before, now they were a hundred times worse.

The goat gobbled their food, and scratched the door, chewed up their boots, and left them unwelcome surprises on the floor. And the noise! The goat bleated and brayed from morning till night, stopping only to sleep. And then it would snore like a boat full of sailors! By the third day, their little house smelled so bad, it was said that folk living on Bickersay could tell when they opened their front door!

The others begged Nessa to get rid of the goat, but she refused. The cailleach had spoken, and who were they to disagree.

Eventually the long week came to an end, and as the sun went down on the seventh day, Nessa's husband and her oldest son loaded the very reluctant goat – because you can imagine he enjoyed living in that house – on to the back of their cart. And with a sigh of relief, they took him back to the shepherd's hut.

Morag passed by the next morning, unsure what to expect. And what she found was the happiest family she had ever seen!

That obnoxious food-gobbling, door-scratching, boot-chewing, floor-peeing, stinky old goat was finally out of their lives! As Nessa poured Morag a cup of tea, she spoke in wonder at the magic the cailleach had performed.

Where once the house had seemed cramped, now it felt like a palace, and those children that had once seemed so noisy now appeared like quiet little angels! Morag was delighted for her friend, but she had a wee concern: what if the magic began to wear off, and Nessa became unhappy again? Nessa smiled and looked over at her sons. The boys had promised to help around the house from now on. They would tidy up and wash the dishes and they would even make their own beds! And if by any chance things did turn bad, she would simply take a walk up to the Wild Goat Place and borrow the shepherd's goat again. Only next time it might have to stay for an entire month!

To all bears, mine especially

Katie Morag
and the Tiresome Ted

There was great excitement on the Isle of Struay. Mrs McColl at the Post Office had had a new baby, and everyone was delighted. Everyone, that is, except Katie Morag. She had been in a bad mood ever since the new baby had arrived.

"No one talks to *me* any more," she grumbled to herself, "or brings *me* presents."

"Don't worry," everyone said knowingly. "Katie Morag will soon get over it."

But Katie Morag could not and would not get over it. She kept doing naughty things, like stamping her feet and nipping her little brother, Liam.

One day she was so cross that she stomped all the way down to the jetty and kicked her friendly old one-eyed teddy bear into the sea.

"Tiresome Ted!" she shouted, as he disappeared into the choppy waves.

Mrs McColl was at her wits' end. "How can I cope with running the Post Office *and* with looking after the new baby *and* Liam, when Katie Morag is behaving like this?" she asked, throwing her arms up in despair.

Mr McColl said that he *was* trying to help.

Grannie Island picked up a basketful of the baby's dirty washing and left, saying they could send Katie Morag over to stay with her, if she became too much of a handful.

That night the first of the winter storms battered at the window. Katie Morag could not sleep. She wondered what had become of her old teddy and she began to wish she hadn't thrown him away.

She crept over to Liam's bed and took
his hot-water bottle . . . but it didn't make
her feel much better.

KATIE MORAG
DELIVERS THE MAIL
Mairi Hedderwick

The next morning things seemed even worse. Katie Morag woke up to a wet bed. Liam thought it was very funny, but Mrs McColl was furious. It was the last straw.

"I think perhaps Katie Morag should go to Grannie Island's for a few days, after all," sighed Mr McColl.

Katie Morag trudged slowly over to Grannie Island's on the other side of the Bay.

"Having bad moods is very tiring," she thought to herself, and so engrossed was she with her own crossness that she didn't notice a familiar object being flung up by the waves of the incoming tide.

The bad weather lasted for two whole days and nights. Grannie Island could not get on with the washing, and Katie Morag was forced to stay indoors. She wondered how everyone was back at home.

And all the while her old teddy bear lay abandoned on the beach in front of Grannie Island's house. He was a sorry sight.

At last, the rain stopped and the sun came out. Katie Morag felt so much better and she decided to stop being in a bad mood. She went down to the high tide-line to collect driftwood for Grannie's stove.

Katie Morag found all sorts of other interesting things that had been washed up by the storm: a ball for Liam, a box for Mr McColl, a bottle for Mrs McColl and a beautiful, big conch shell.

"I'll give this to the new baby," thought Katie Morag,
"and show her how to hear the sea."

It was only then that Katie Morag noticed the two furry arms sticking up through the seaweed. She couldn't believe her eyes. Old Ted wasn't lost, after all.

Katie Morag rushed back to Grannie's and dried her teddy out by the stove. She filled his tummy with some fluffy sheep's wool and then laboriously began sewing up the large tear in his tummy.

Buttons

But even with his new eye on, he still looked the worse for the wear. When Grannie Island wasn't looking, Katie Morag took something out of the washing-basket.

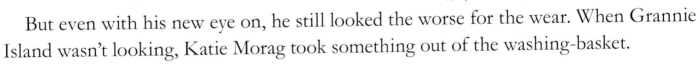

The journey back to the Post Office seemed to take ages. Katie Morag couldn't wait to get home to show everyone the things she had found down by the shore.

The other islanders were pleased to see Katie Morag looking like
her old self again. "She's got over it," they all said, nodding their heads.

"Thank you for the lovely presents, Katie Morag," said Mrs McColl.
"And thank you, Grannie Island, for doing all that washing."

"It's good to have our Katie Morag back, and to see Old Ted again," said Mr McColl, smiling.

"I'll never, ever throw him away again, or call him Tiresome Ted," said Katie Morag, and she meant it.

And nobody said a thing about the missing Babygro from Mrs McColl's washing-basket, which was perhaps just as well.

Hugh Handy

A folk tale told at Grannie Island's Ceilidh by the Lady Author

Long ago there was a famous boat builder on Struay who lived at the Port of the Man. When he was born he was given two first names, just like Katie Morag. He was called Hugh Andy. But when he grew up, he was called Hugh Handy, because he was so good at making things – boats, especially. They were so well built he became the Famous Master Boat Builder of Struay. This is also the story of how he got his final nickname, Hugh Handy the Man, and how the bay beside his workshop was named the Port of the Man.

The ruins of the Deserted Village are nearby. Everyone in Struay lived there, long ago – before the present day Village and School and Village Hall were built. Er, wait a minute something's missing? The Shop and Post Office, of course! The most important building on Struay.

Everyone had boats in those times. The Struachs would often sail over to visit friends and relatives on the neighbouring islands of Fuay, Coll and Tiree. Nobody ever went to the Island of Bickersay, because the people who lived there were very argumentative! On still summer's nights, when the sea was silky smooth, you could hear voices. "That's them arguing again!" some folk on Struay would say. "No, they're having a party!" said others. "So long as they don't come here!" said everyone.

As Hugh Handy's reputation spread, he got lots of orders to make more boats. He decided to look for a young apprentice to help him. Maxi Ina, who was just leaving school, wanted to be the next boat builder on Struay. Girls never made boats and her mother was stunned but pleased when Hugh Handy agreed. Meanwhile, over the sea, the Bickersay men got jealous of Hugh Handy's reputation because they thought they built the best boats.

They sent a passing seagull with a message for Hugh Handy to say that they were coming to challenge him. When Hugh Handy got the message he was worried. He had never boasted about his boats, or himself.

Master craftsmen have special clothes to wear on important occasions: a velvet cloak, a feathered hat and a big gold chain. Hugh Handy never wore his and they hung on a hook in the workshop, gathering dust. Hugh Handy had a plan and explained it to a wide-eyed Maxi Ina, as the flotilla of Bickersay boats appeared on the horizon.

He told Maxi Ina that she was to pretend to be the master and he would pretend to be the apprentice. He took his cloak, hat and chain off the hook and told Maxi Ina to put them on. Hugh Handy told her to politely welcome the Bickersay men. They would think she was the master, of course. And then he told her what to say if they challenged her.

The Bickersay men were soon surfing ashore, colliding and barging into each other. The port became littered with broken boats and oars. Maxi Ina walked regally towards them. "Welcome," she said.

The biggest Bickersay man rudely ignored her politeness, and shouted, "We have come to challenge YOU for the title of the Best Boat Builder in the Western Isles!"

"As you say," replied Maxi Ina. "But I suggest you have a competition with my apprentice, first."

"Easy peasy!" scoffed the big bully, looking at Hugh Handy, and seeing how shabby he was in his work clothes.

"Show them, Apprentice, how you will put the legs on that stool you are making," said Maxi Ina, in a very superior voice. She was enjoying herself!

Hugh Handy carefully balanced the carved wooden seat, which had a hole at each corner, on top of four separate wooden legs. He then took four wooden pegs, which would normally be hammered into the seat, and joined everything together. He put them in his pocket.

The Bickersay men burst out laughing. "Anybody can put a stool together!"

Hugh Handy left the work table, and walked to the far end of the workshop. He flung one of the wooden pegs the length of the room. It curved up in the air and flew directly down into one of the seat holes, firmly joining up with the leg underneath, without having to be hammered in!

"If the apprentice is as skilful as that, then the master must be doubly skilled," the Bickersay men muttered.

"I think we should go home," said the biggest Bickersay man, feeling rather small.

"But our boats are all smashed up!" said the second biggest Bickersay man.

But kindly Hugh Handy had an idea. "Why don't we build one big boat, all together, and that will take you home?" And so it was decided.

"What a man Hugh Handy is!" all the Struay Islanders whispered. But everyone knew they had to keep the secret until the Bickersay men left.

Maxi Ina had a grand time ordering everyone about. But it was Hugh Handy who shared his skills with the Bickersay men. They learned a lot. When the magnificent boat with a beautiful mermaid carved on the bow was launched, the Bickersay men thanked the master and the apprentice, and said they would be back next year. Not for a challenge, but for a ceilidh!

"We've heard that the best ceilidhs are on Struay . . . We'll bring our wives, and our children!"

Hugh Handy and Maxi Ina, and all the Islanders, heaved a big sigh of relief when the boat full of happily waving Bickersay men disappeared round the headland. Although Maxi Ina had enjoyed being the master, she was glad to take off the heavy cloak, the hat and the chain.

"But I'll have to wear them next year when they come back, won't I?" she said, cheekily, to Hugh Handy.

"Aye, but you have a bit more to learn before then," smiled Hugh Handy the Man.

The
Hermit's
Hut

Mr McColl's bad moods were always at the end of the month. Not only had he to do all the accounts for the Isle of Struay Shop and Post Office, he also had to visit his brother, Matthew, who lived on the other side of the island.

Mrs McColl refused to visit her brother-in-law.

Matthew was a hermit and lived in a hut. "That hut is just like a midden inside!" exclaimed Mrs McColl. "Decent folks don't live like that!"

Matthew never came to the Village, or at least the last time he had come was so long ago nobody was sure it had ever happened. Everyone came to the Village on boat days. "Even hermits, sometimes," exclaimed the islanders, "to get supplies, surely?"

Katie Morag knew what a hermit was. It was someone who didn't like people around and didn't like going anywhere. And hermits always lived on their own, but in a different way from Grannie Island. Grannie Island lived all alone but she was forever having friends and visitors in and out of her house and popping over to the Village on her old grey tractor to see the McColls and the Shop and Post Office.

All Matthew wanted was to be left alone and to keep his whereabouts unknown. Mr McColl, however, said it was his duty to go once a month and check that his brother was all right.

At the end of this particular month the weather was wet and windy. Mr McColl put on his walking boots and groaned.

Katie Morag and Liam had had to play inside all that morning on account of the weather and now they were very bored with each other. When Katie Morag gets fed up with people she likes to be on her own. She gets her paints out and then forgets all the horrible things that have happened.

When Liam gets fed up he loves to pester and PESTER his big sister . . .

"Go AWAY!" screamed Katie Morag, as Liam emptied all the stickle bricks over her sheet of paper and smudged the wet paint.

"WHAT IS GOING ON?" Mrs McColl was in a bad mood too. "This room is a MIDDEN!" she shrieked. "What am I going to do with you? What a worry you are! Get it tidy AT ONCE! And then, you, Katie Morag," she added, "put your boots on and go over to Matthew's with your father."

"I bet no one tells Uncle Matthew to tidy up his room and I bet he's got no wee brother who spoils everything," thought Katie Morag, angrily.

Hermit's Hut

Boorachy Bog

Queer Quarry

Castle McColl

Deserted Village

Fossil Cave

The Bad Step

Graveyard

Eagle Rock

Lobster Pt.

The pickup bounced along the track behind the Village and past the peat banks where the islanders dug for fuel in the spring. Out to sea, Katie Morag could see Lobster Point where the biggest lobsters were found in the summer and then she saw the ruined walls of the Deserted Village behind which the sheep sheltered in the winter. Up the hill beyond stood the scary high walls of ancient Castle McColl.

Mr McColl pointed out all these things to her. He told stories about the Clan McColl whose Chief, Rory of the Flaming Red Beard, had lived in the Castle long ago and was her ancestor. Mr McColl was a great storyteller.

Then he started to sing, "Heigh Ho! Heigh Ho! It's off to the Hut we go! I like having you aboard, Katie Morag!"

Katie Morag was wondering, however, if she should have stayed at home. What would Uncle Matthew look like? What would he say? What would he DO when he saw her coming as well?

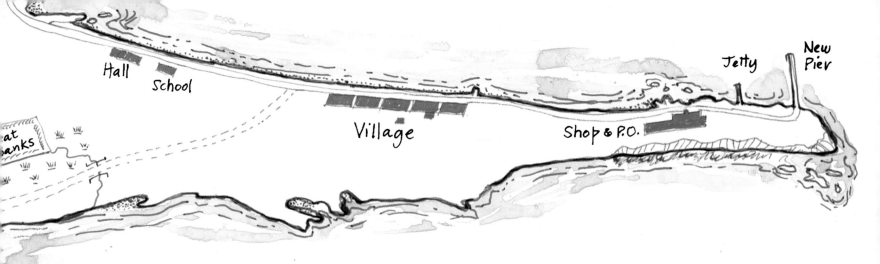

They left the pickup at the old graveyard nearby the Queer Quarry and started to scramble up and over the Bad Step, past the Fossil Cave way down deep below the cliffs that looked out to sea over the Fathomless Depths.

When they got to the Boorachy Bog, Katie Morag was very glad of her Wellington boots. It was an adventurous journey.

They were getting nearer and nearer to the Hermit's Hut. Soon they were there.

Mrs McColl was all wrong. Admittedly, the inside of the Hut was very full and cluttered and a cockerel was standing on top of a pile of dishes in the sink but it could never be called a midden. Everything looked very interesting even though half of it was on the floor. "Highest shelf in the house," Mrs McColl always said. But it made sense to Katie Morag – much easier to find things that way.

"Matthew! You are a slovenly disgrace to the McColl family!" cried Mr McColl, shaking his head at his brother. "What am I going to do with you? What a worry you are!"

"I don't worry about you," replied Matthew quietly. He saw Katie Morag peeking behind her father's back.

"What do you think, Katie Morag?"

Uncle Matthew was nothing like Katie Morag remembered, or imagined she remembered. He did look a bit strange with straggly scruffy hair over his eyes. But she often looked like that. He spoke very gently and he wasn't going to DO anything awful – that was obvious.

He was very preoccupied.

On the table were lots of brushes and pots of colours and all around, the walls – the actual walls – were covered with pictures showing all the things that Katie Morag had seen on the journey that afternoon. Mrs McColl would never allow her to do that on her bedroom wall . . .

"I think you like being on your own," she answered, bravely. She understood.

Whilst Mr McColl shooed out the cockerel Uncle Matthew took Katie Morag into his garden. Strawberries were fat and juicy on their stalks. Raspberries and loganberries swelled from branches. Apples and pears groaned from trees. Every variety of fruit and vegetable was there for the picking. Honey bees buzzed in and out of hives and the cockerel's hens laid more eggs than they could cope with. A brown and white goat popped her head over the fence.

Of course Matthew didn't have to go to the Village for supplies!

And there was the real midden. It was very tidy. The cockerel was atop, showing off.

Matthew went back into the Hut smiling a special goodbye smile to Katie Morag. Her pockets were full of strawberries.

" I would like to visit Uncle Matthew again," she told her dad as they set off homewards . . .

Mr McColl smiled. "I think that would be very fine," he replied.

"I'm going to help him with his wall painting. I'll paint you and me walking along the cliffs above the Fossil Cave." Katie Morag was excited.

Perhaps it wasn't so bad having a hermit in the family after all.

"I think Uncle Matthew is magic and I think it is best that his whereabouts are unknown," stated Katie Morag.

She looked forward to the end of next month. And the next. Not only would she see Uncle Matthew again, she would also have her dad all to herself on the long journey over to the Hermit's Hut. It had been a great day after all.

The Gardens of Struay

Everyone grows something on the Isle of Struay. Well, nearly everyone . . .
Mrs Bayview wins the prize at the Show for the greatest variety of
flowers. Sometimes Mrs Bayview gets lost in her garden. So do her tools.

Mr MacMaster, the farmer at High Farm, says a garden is far too small
for him. He plants fields and fields of tatties and turnips, cabbages
and carrots. He has to make sure the fences are strong.

The Lady Artist has a sculpture garden. The sculptures don't grow but my, the grass certainly does!

Neilly Beag has a window box. In it he grows chives and parsley, fennel and mint, thyme, camomile, lavender and rosemary. Neilly Beag chops herbs into his soups and stews. And his teapot.

Katie Morag, quite contrary
How does your garden grow?
With cockle shells and silver bells
And pretty maids all in a row!

Dainty cowries, clams and mussels
No need to weed or mow!
No aching back or blistered hands
It's off to the shore I go!

Castle McColl

Katie Morag McColl's two cats spend most of their time sleeping and stretching, comfy and cuddly on the top of Katie Morag's bed. When the moon is full, however, they go wandering. For days and nights. No one knows where they go. They like it that way. Eventually, with the aid of the great full moon they find their way home.

Fabbydoo is large and a golden gingery red colour. Mr Mistake is smaller and pure white all over. He has one poor eye that can't see a thing but Fabbydoo looks after him. They are great friends.

But not with the Big Boy Cousins. When the Big Boy Cousins come for their holidays to the island they tease Fabbydoo and Mr Mistake. The cats jump off the cosy cushions and hope that the moon is full.

"Here they come! Hide! Hide!" Katie Morag warned Fabbydoo and Mr Mistake one day. The boat had arrived with all the holiday people and there were the Cousins disembarking with their camping gear.

As long as her cats were hiding safe, Katie Morag loved it when the Big Boy Cousins came to stay. They pitched their tent at Grannie Island's and Katie Morag was allowed to take her sleeping bag over and camp too. It was good knowing that Grannie was nearby – especially in the middle of the night.

"It's different this time," declared Hector, the biggest Boy Cousin.
"We are pitching the tent by the Castle! It's boring over at Grannie Island's."

What Hector really meant was that the usual site was too close to Grannie
Island. There she could keep too much of an eye on them. Once Katie Morag
and the Big Boy Cousins got together they got up to all sorts of mischief.

"Please can I go? PLEASE!" Katie Morag implored her parents.

Castle McColl was a long way away from the Village. "Oh! All right," said
her father. "As long as you promise to tell them all about Clan Chief Rory
McColl of the Flaming Red Beard and the Wee White One-Eyed Ghost . . ."

The Big Boy Cousins could have done without Katie Morag dragging
behind and maybe getting homesick in the middle of the night, but stories
about Clan Chief Rory McColl and the Wee White One-Eyed Ghost
sounded interesting.

After all, they were McColls, too . . .

Castle McColl was ancient. Nobody had lived in it for years and years.
Just the pigeons, the mice and a bat or two. Long ago it had been a lively
place full of chieftains and warriors, maidens, servants and deerhounds.
And the Clan Chief Rory of the Flaming Red Beard. And the Wee White
One-Eyed Ghost – if Mr McColl was to be believed . . .

It was very exciting to pitch the tent beside such history, said Hector, pompously, as everyone busied themselves setting up camp. Katie Morag helped Jamie gather old timber from the Castle for the fire. He wanted to hear the stories about the Castle straight away.

"No!" said Katie Morag, a bit bossily. "Once we have had our supper and it is time to go to bed. THAT is the time for stories . . ." She enjoyed knowing something the others did not.

"Bedtime stories! Pah!" sneered Hector after they had gorged on sausages and beans, Grannie Island's apple pie and gallons of juice. Hector was a bit bad-tempered. There hadn't been enough sausages. He was sure some were missing.

"Yeah!" said Archie. "Try catching me going to bed! I'm going to stay up all night!" The cousins cheered and raced off into the empty gloomy Castle, except for Jamie who felt a bit sorry for Katie Morag and stayed behind.

BUY
BULK
BEANS

JUICE

"Come and tell us the stories in HERE! Katie Morag," the others teased and taunted, through the arrow slit windows.

Katie Morag wasn't sure about that. Maybe neither was Jamie. They both wished Grannie Island was nearby. It was beginning to get dark. A big cheesy full moon was coming up over the sea. The glow from the campfire was warm and the sleeping bags in the tent were looking so cosy . . .

But she wasn't going to let the Big Boy Cousins – or Jamie – know she was frightened.

"Come on!" she said to Jamie and ran as fast as she could into the Castle.

The Big Boy Cousins were hiding, calling with echoey voices from shadowy corners, "Yoo Whoo-oo! Yoo Whoo-oo! Katie Morag and Jamie are afraid of Big Chief Flaming Red Beard and the Wee White One-Eyed Ghost! Fearties! Fearties!"

"We are NOT!" shouted back Katie Morag, riled. "Ready or not, we're coming to get you!"

Everything went silent. The Castle was very scary and eerie. The light coming in through the tiny windows was dim . . . Katie Morag and Jamie held hands and crept the long length of the corridor, their other hands feeling the way along the slimy walls.

Suddenly there was a shrieking and yelling and a blubbering from above. Hector, Archie, Dougal and Murdo Iain came stumbling and clattering down the spiral staircase, terrified out of their wits.

"The Beard! The Beard! It's cut off and it's growling!" screamed Hector as he flew past, heading for the entrance to the Castle.

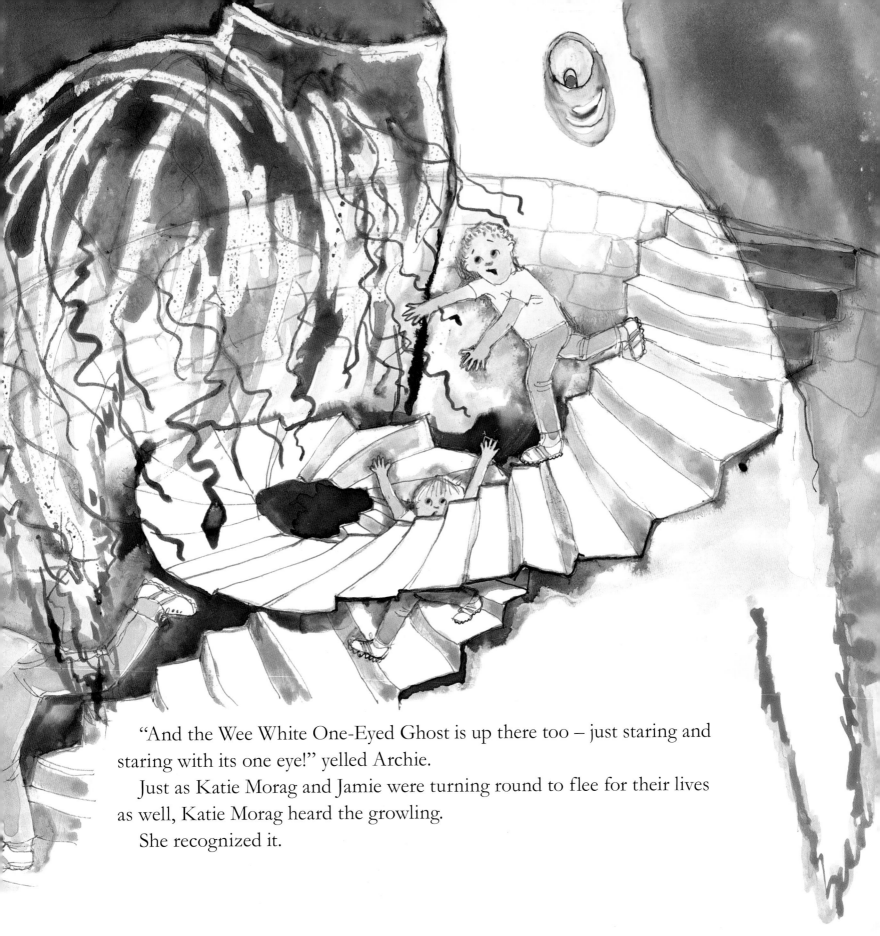

"And the Wee White One-Eyed Ghost is up there too – just staring and staring with its one eye!" yelled Archie.

Just as Katie Morag and Jamie were turning round to flee for their lives as well, Katie Morag heard the growling.

She recognized it.

Letting go of Jamie's tugging hand she found her way up the darkening staircase to the room above. There in a shadowy corner WAS a big gingery red hairy lump of a thing, very like a cut-off beard. And it WAS growling . . .

It was Fabbydoo chewing his way through a string of sausages!!

Fabbydoo always growls when he is happy. So does Mr Mistake. So guess who was the Wee White One-Eyed Ghost staring and staring, waiting patiently for his share?

"Oh! Fabbydoo and Mr Mistake, aren't you wonderful!" whispered Katie Morag, giving them each a cuddle. "See you back home at the end of the full moon – and the camping holiday!" Then she carefully found her way down the dark stairs and along the even darker corridor to the outside of the Castle. The dark blue sky was full of stars.

The Big Boy Cousins were huddled in their sleeping bags in the tent, still terrified by their experience, amazed at Katie Morag's bravery. She decided not to tell them about Fabbydoo and Mr Mistake.

"Now it's time for bedtime stories," she said.

"No thank you!" replied the Big Boy Cousins, scaredly, and rolled over to sleep.

Katie Morag sat for a while looking out of the tent flap at the moon, the stars and the silhouette of Castle McColl before she snuggled down to sleep. She could hear Mr Mistake's growl . . . Good, she thought, it was his turn now to get a share of the sausages.

Then she thought she might tell Jamie in the morning about the real Flaming Red Beard and the real Wee White One-Eyed Ghost. But only if he could keep the secret . . .

Footprints on the Beach

Someone hasn't been
on the sand – yet!
I wonder who?

Stone Soup

A folk tale told at Grannie Island's Ceilidh by Mrs McColl

Most folk in the olden days were very poor, but they worked hard and got by. But one year disaster struck, and the reason was tatties: potatoes.

The tatties got sick, so people couldn't eat them. No tatties meant no food, and everyone became very, very hungry indeed. One of those hungry souls was a young lad from Ullapool named Calum MacAulay. Calum had no family or a home to call his own, so he wandered the country looking for food and shelter.

One day, near Ardnamurchan, he spotted an old boat abandoned on the beach. Calum was starving, so he decided to row across to the big island of Mull and try his luck there.

Calum was a kind boy, and handsome too, with bright green eyes and a lovely smile. And though he'd hardly been to school, he was as clever a lad as you could ever meet. But Calum was a rotten sailor, and instead of rowing south to Mull, he headed west. After a while Calum began to panic, thinking he'd have to row all the way to America, but finally he caught sight of a pretty wee island with five tall mountains along the top of it; and that island was Struay!

At last Calum reached the shore and he set off along the path until
he came to the village.

He went up to the very first door and knocked on it. Now, people in
the old days were normally kind, but in these hard times they were wary of
strangers. Eventually, a young woman came to the door; a pretty girl by the
name of Fiona. Calum said he was sorry to trouble her, but did she have a
crust of bread, or a handful of oats he could have. Fiona felt sorry for Calum,
but explained that they were a poor family, and didn't have anything to spare.

He thanked her anyway, and went on to the next house, where he heard
the exact same story: times were hard.

Calum was about to give up, when he spotted an old iron pot lying near the village well, and that's when he had an idea. He washed the pot out, filled it with water, and built a little fire and put the water on to boil. And then he started looking for a rock. His search went on for quite a while: some stones were too big, some too small, some too round, others not quite round enough.

And then, finally, he found the perfect one, and he rinsed it in the well and plopped it in the pot. There were no TVs and computers then, so if folk wanted entertainment, they looked out of their windows. And that's exactly what everyone was doing! Staring at this mysterious stranger, boiling up a pot of water with nothing in it except a rock!

Fiona was the first to come out: she was desperate to know what on earth he was up to. So she walked right up to him, and asked.

"Well, surely it's obvious," Calum replied. "I'm making a lovely big pot of stone soup."

"Stone soup! I've never heard of such a thing," she replied.

"Well, you don't know what you're missing," Calum said. "I've eaten roast beef in Orkney, and pies in Dundee, pork chops in Glasgow and cheese in Tiree. But there's not a dish in the whole of Scotland as delicious as stone soup."

Fiona looked at him in amazement.

Calum looked at the pot and sighed. "Of course, to make it absolutely perfect, I should really add a little something – a carrot maybe . . . Still, it'll be fine the way it is."

Fiona thought for a moment, and then she spoke up. "Well, um . . . I might have a couple of carrots."

"Well," Calum said, "that would be a treat, right enough, and when the soup's made, I'll share it with you."

So Fiona fetched her carrots, and Calum added them to the soup. As he and Fiona sat watching the pot simmer, a few more people came out of their houses. Calum smiled at them, and tasted a spoonful of the broth. "Mmm," he said, "as good a stone soup as I've ever tasted! Of course, some sliced-up onion would add a finishing touch, but I mustn't be greedy."

At that, an old woman announced that she had a small bag of onions. If Calum were to share the soup with her and her family, she'd gladly add them to the mix. The onions were added, and a short while later, Calum declared it the finest broth in the whole of the Hebrides!

By this time, the entire village was gathered round the large pot, and they had to admit that the stone soup was smelling very fine indeed.

But one of the neighbours said, "Maybe a wee bit of ham wouldn't do any harm."

"Oh, no indeed," said Calum. "In fact, the people of the Borders are known for adding ham to their stone soup."

"Well then," said the neighbour, "I might have a few slices," and in they went. They all wanted to add something now. Some brought beans, others had peas, garlic – all manner of wonderful things. After two hours, Calum declared the stone soup was well and truly ready.

Everyone rushed back into their houses, and emerged with bowls and spoons of all shapes and sizes. They filled their bowls, and filled them again, until there wasn't one single drop left. Then someone found a fiddle, and they danced and danced till the sun went down.

In the years that followed, if you asked folk on Struay to name their favourite food, you would only get one answer. "Why . . . stone soup, of course. All you need is a pot of water and a nice round stone . . . though you can add a bit of this and a bit of that, if you're feeling fancy."

Calum decided to stay on Struay. He'd taken a liking to Fiona, and she to him.

Soon they were married, and every Sunday he would make a great big delicious pot of stone soup, with that very same rock he used the first day they met.

It was always enough to feed them and their seven children!
The rock was passed down to their oldest daughter, and she passed
it on to hers, until eventually it came to Grannie Island! Because Calum
was her great-great-great-grandfather.

For Kirsty, Erika and Elizabeth, Stronvar and Port na Luing

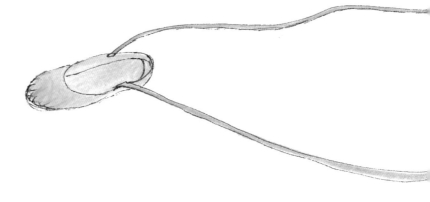

Katie Morag
and the Dancing Class

ISLE of STRUAY
SHOP & POST OFFICE

OPENING
HOURS:

WHEN
THE BOAT
COMES IN
(WEATHER
PERMITTING)

SATURDAY
DANCING
CLASSES
BALLET
10.00AM
TAP
11.00AM
VILLAGE HALL

Bistro

OBAN TIMES
AIRPORT
FOR
STRUAY
- HOPES
&
FEARS

It was decided that it would be a good thing for the children on the Isle of Struay to have dancing lessons.

Agnes, Fay, Sasha and the Big Boy Cousins were keen to start, especially when they heard that Mrs Mackie would provide juice and biscuits at the end of each lesson.

The boys chose tap and the girls ballet. But Katie Morag McColl said she had better things to do on a Saturday morning – like getting a backy on her mother's Post Office bike or checking the lobster creels with Neilly Beag.

But Grannie Island said that ballet would be good for Katie Morag's co-ordination. Granma Mainland had already ordered pink pumps and a leotard from a dance shop on the Mainland. She was also sewing a frilly frou-frou skirt. She longed to see her granddaughter in a pretty outfit instead of that old jumper and skirt and those dreadful wellies.

Katie Morag loved her wellies.

She dreaded the thought of ballet lessons, but
it had all been decided by the two grandmothers.

On the first Saturday, Katie Morag reluctantly put on the leotard. Granma Mainland rushed into Katie Morag's bedroom waving a cloud of frills. The frou-frou skirt!

"Oh, no . . . !" thought Katie Morag. But, "Thank you very much, Granma Mainland," she said.

"Hurry up! Don't be late! There is to be a Dance Performance on Show Day! You will look SO pretty!" smiled Granma Mainland.

ISLE of STRUAY

157

Katie Morag headed unwillingly towards the Village Hall. It was boat day and all the villagers were at the pier. But all was not silent and deserted at the last house in the Village. Nurse's gate was wide open and a flock of sheep were in her garden, baa-ing delightedly as they feasted on her early lettuces.

Katie Morag tried to chase them out but *every* time they came back in before she could close the gate.

After a long time, and a lot of shouting, which she enjoyed, Katie Morag finally got the sheep out and firmly shut the gate.

Katie Morag was late for ballet class . . .

On the second Saturday, Katie Morag decided to walk to the Village Hall along the shore. There had been a big storm in the night. She was on the lookout for anything interesting washed up on the tide line.

Once she had found a Frisbee which she gave to Liam for his birthday. And then there was the terrible time when she had been in a bad mood and had kicked her old teddy into the sea. She was so lucky to find him washed up two days later near Grannie Island's house.

This particular day, there was nothing special on the tide line –
but Katie Morag just *had* to keep on looking.

Katie Morag was *very* late for ballet class . . .

On the third Saturday, Flora Ann screamed all through breakfast. It being boat day, Katie Morag very kindly offered to stay with her until Mr and Mrs McColl collected the mail and supplies for the Shop and Post Office from the pier.

WIPE YOUR FEET

Welcome

For once Katie Morag didn't mind having to look after her baby sister. Grannie Island was downstairs wiping the shelves in the Shop and completely forgot it was Dancing Class day. Katie Morag didn't remind her. The boat was an hour late in arriving.

Katie Morag was *extremely* late for ballet class.

SO LATE that she missed the whole class. Agnes, Fay and Sasha had already gone home. The Big Boy Cousins were putting on their tap shoes.

"What is it like to tap dance?" Katie Morag asked.

"It's like playing the drums with your feet," replied Hector, Archie, Dougal, Jamie and Murdo Iain, clacking the metal-studded toes and heels of their shoes on the floor.

WHAT A NOISE!

Katie Morag copied them with her wellies but the sound was like a wet fish flapping in the bottom of Neilly Beag's boat.

"You have to have the metal bits," laughed Jamie.

Mrs Mackie had been listening. "Would you like to come to tap, Katie Morag, instead of ballet? I am sure Granma Mainland would get you the shoes."

Katie Morag desperately wanted to say "Yes, please!" but she couldn't *possibly* ask Granma Mainland for more dancing shoes.

That night Katie Morag was staying over at Grannie Island's.

Wearily, she told Grannie Island the whole sad story.

"Take off your wellies," sighed Grannie Island sympathetically, "and have a rest by the fire."

Katie Morag looked at her wellies. "All they need are bits of metal . . ." she said forlornly.

Grannie Island suddenly started rummaging in a cupboard. She held up a pair of dusty leather boots. "My old tackety boots!"

"Silly Grannie!" scoffed Katie Morag, a bit rudely. "They are FAR TOO BIG!"

But Grannie Island was levering the metal tacks from their soles and hammering them onto the soles of Katie Morag's wellies.

On the fourth Saturday, on the dot of 11 o'clock, Katie Morag was the first at the door of the Hall. Mrs Mackie said not a word about the rather unusual tap shoes.

"What are you like, Katie Morag?" the Big Boy Cousins groaned. But Jamie laughed. "She's like she is. She's Katie Morag!"

Katie Morag worked really hard to catch up on her cousins.
Rehearsals had already started for the Dance Performance on Show Day.
Mrs Mackie made them practise their routine over and over again.

On the evening of the Dance Performance,
the islanders packed into the Village Hall.
The two grandmothers were in the front row;
Granma Mainland dressed up in all her finery,
looking forward to seeing Katie Morag in *her* finery . . .

Granma Mainland was so disappointed when she saw Katie Morag wearing that old jumper and skirt and those dreadful wellies – *on the stage!*

But when Katie Morag danced perfectly in time with the Big Boy Cousins and even did a solo turn in her tackety wellies, Granma Mainland had to admit that she was extremely impressed.

Katie Morag was equally impressed by the ballet performance. Agnes was Aladdin, in a blue satin bolero and baggy trousers, and Sasha was Princess Jasmine in veils of purple silk. Fay performed high wild kicks as the Genie coming out of the lamp.

At the end of the wonderful evening, the Lady Artist thanked Mrs Mackie for all her hard work and gave her a bouquet of flowers specially ordered from the Mainland.

"And I would like to thank all the dancers who worked so very hard, too," Mrs Mackie replied. "Katie Morag worked the hardest of them all!"

EXIT

Afterwards, Katie Morag apologized to Granma Mainland for not telling her about missing ballet lessons and how she really liked tap dancing.

Then she said, "But Granma Mainland, I think I would like to go to both classes next year . . ."

Granma Mainland smiled her forgiveness. Maybe she would see Katie Morag in that frilly frou-frou skirt one day, after all.

"And, look," said Katie Morag brightly, "the ballet shoes I didn't use this year won't be wasted. They will make cosy liners for my wellies in the winter!"

Annie Jessie and the Merboy

A folk tale told at Grannie Island's Ceilidh by Uncle Matthew

Long ago, on the Isle of Struay, there lived a teenage girl called Annie Jessie. And she was born in a house on the headland beyond the new pier, which has a lovely view of the Isle of Fuay. When Annie Jessie was young she had to look after her brothers and sisters, as her mother had sadly died. Her father was a teacher on the island, and he was away all day at the school. When he got back home with the older children, he expected the house to be clean and tidy and an evening meal on the table. Not only did Annie Jessie have to look after the family, she also had to look after the cow, the pig, the hens, the sheep, the dogs and the cats. And after breakfast, her father would go off to school. And Annie Jessie, after she had fed all the animals, would go to the peat bank, with the little ones, and collect fuel for the stove. Finally, at the end of the day, once all the children were asleep, and with her father working at the table, she would row out into the bay to catch fish for the next day's breakfast and supper.

One particular evening it was wild weather. Annie Jessie sheltered behind
the boat tied up on the shore, waiting for the storm to pass. She listened to
the wind roaring and screeching around her. But there was another sound,
like someone crying. Annie Jessie stumbled over the slippery seaweed and saw
the most amazing sight! Now I'm sure you all know what a Mermaid is, but
what she saw was a Merboy. He was right in front of her, sitting on a rock with
tears streaming down his face! Annie Jessie asked him why he was so upset.
The Merboy wailed that he had lost his comb and that the Sea King would
be furious. "He's in charge of all us sea creatures, you know, and can be very
fierce. We Merboys and Mermaids must comb our hair twice a day."

"I'll get you another comb," Annie Jessie promised. "I'll bring it tomorrow."

And the Merboy smiled for the first time – such a lovely smile – and disappeared into the foaming waves with a happy flip of his tail.

How was Annie Jessie to get a comb? There was only one comb in her house and that was needed every morning for all the family, and it was often lost. As she wandered back along the shore she saw some long, flat razor shells and put them in her pocket. But that night Annie Jessie couldn't sleep. Feeling cold and lonely, she remembered her promise to the Merboy and remembered the razor shells in her pocket. Her fishing knife was sharp and it wouldn't take long to carve one of those long, flat shells. So she lit a candle and sat close to the light. But the shell was brittle, and soon broke in two.

The second, third and fourth shells all shattered too. Dawn was breaking, and when she got to the last shell, the candle guttered out.

In the half-light of the skylight window, Annie Jessie worked ever so carefully. And this time, she made the most beautiful comb. She carved some hearts and kisses on it before racing down to the shore.

"Merboy, here is your new comb," Annie Jessie called out.

"Thank you," he smiled, as he took it from her. "It is beautiful . . . and so are you."

Annie Jessie smiled. She thought he was beautiful too! The Merboy told Annie Jessie to untie the boat and follow him, and he would find her the very best fish and would continue to do so, from that moment on. Being with the Merboy was the best part of the day for Annie Jessie, and the family had mounds of fried fish for breakfast, and colossal fish pies for supper!

Grateful though she was to the Merboy, she knew he could not help her with her other chores. And when the weather was too bad for fishing, she would sit beside him on the rocks, and tell him how lonely and exhausted she sometimes got, and how she wished she could have a life with him. "Would you really like to live with me?" asked the Merboy hopefully, as he had had the same thought!

Now the Sea King had heard about their romance, and decided to do something about it. A large, rolling wave was far out to sea, and as it came close to land, it turned into a team of white horses, with foaming manes pulling a huge shell chariot towards the shore. The Sea King stood tall and fierce.

He boomed out his message: "A little seabird has told me you have fallen in love and want to be together." Annie Jessie and the Merboy agreed wholeheartedly. But Annie Jessie knew she could not leave her family, and told the Sea King so.

"They will be fine," bellowed the Sea King. "I will send a new teacher to Struay, who will help your father at the school, and at home . . . and I will make you a beautiful place to live."

And so saying, he turned to the sea and raised his hands. The setting sun darkened, and suddenly it was deepest night.

Thunder and lightning grumbled and flashed, and Annie Jessie and the Merboy huddled together on the rocks! "Look!" commanded the Sea King, pointing to the horizon. Where there had been dark sea a moment before, there was now a small island, bathed in sunlight!

"This is your island," announced the Sea King.

And so it was that Annie Jessie and the Merboy went to live on the island. And what do you think they called it? They called it the Isle of Fuay!

One fine evening, Annie Jessie met the new Lady Teacher, who was helping her father dig up the tatties. "I like it here," smiled the Lady Teacher. Well, Annie Jessie's brothers and sisters all cheered! Annie Jessie made razor-shell combs for all the family and the Lady Teacher, and a spare one for the Merboy, just in case he lost his special one! And that is the story of the Isle of Fuay.

To all who cope with temptation

Katie Morag
and the Big Boy Cousins

It was the second fortnight in July, and Katie Morag's Big Boy Cousins had arrived from the Mainland to camp at Grannie Island's, as they did each summer.

"Oh, no!" sighed the islanders. "Here they come AGAIN!"
The Big Boy Cousins were very wild and unruly. Katie Morag thought they were wonderful.

"Why do you put up with them, Grannie Island?" exclaimed Mr and Mrs McColl.

"Because nobody else will have them!" declared Grannie Island. "And I could do with some help with the chores."

Grannie Island loaded the provisions into her tractor and trailer, ready for the long, bumpy journey back to her house on the other side of the Bay.

BULK MARSH MALLOWS

Aug 1st
65th
Annual Show

EARLY
ENTRIES
PLEASE

& P.O.

"Coming, Katie Morag?"
smiled the biggest Boy Cousin called Hector.

Soon the tent was pitched and the stores unloaded.

"Now," called Grannie Island. "There are potatoes to be dug up, peats to be fetched and driftwood to be gathered. Who is doing what?"

"GEE WHILICKERS!" groaned Hector, Archie, Dougal,
Jamie and Murdo Iain.

Everyone pretended not to hear Grannie Island, even Katie Morag.
"Hide down by the shore!" whispered Hector.

"It's boring here," moaned Archie, after a while.

"We'll go to the Village, then, and play Chickenelly," said Hector.

"Yeah!" chorused all the Big Boy Cousins – except for Murdo Iain.

"It's an awful long walk," he whined.

"I know a quick way," chirped up Katie Morag.

GLASGOW

She was enjoying being naughty and continued
to ignore Grannie Island's cries for help.

In the Village all was calm and peaceful.
The villagers were inside their houses, having
a well-earned rest after a morning's hard work.
Nobody noticed Grannie Island's heavily
laden boat, heading across the Bay.

195

Chickenelly was a daring game.

"Last one gets caught!" whispered Hector, as he led all the cousins on tiptoe round the gable end of Nurse's house.

Katie Morag's tummy tickled inside with excitement.

Then the Big Boy Cousins, with Katie Morag close on their heels, ran as fast as greased lightning, the length of the Village, banging very loudly on each back door.

BANG – a – BANG – a – BANG – a – BANG – a – BANG!

In their mad rush to get to the safety of the other end of the village houses, they knocked into all sorts of things, and nobody saw Grannie Island racing round the head of the Bay on her tractor.

"And just WHAT do you think you are all up to?" Grannie Island was colossal with fury.

"Chickenelly," said Katie Morag, timidly, wishing she had never heard of the game.

"Gee whilickers!" groaned Hector, Archie, Dougal, Jamie and Murdo Iain.

GREENPEACE

Grannie Island made them all apologize to the upset villagers
and told them to clear up the mess they had caused.

"And you can all WALK back when you are finished!" she shouted.

Even though Grannie Island was angry outside, Katie Morag knew
her Grannie was sad inside, and that made Katie Morag feel sad, too.

Tired and very hungry, the Big Boy Cousins were silent on the long journey
back to Grannie Island's.

Katie Morag walked as fast as she could.

"We've got to say sorry to Grannie," she said.
"*And* help her with the chores."

"Gee whilickers!" groaned Hector, Archie, Dougal,
Jamie *and* Murdo Iain.

The chores didn't take that long once everyone lent a hand.
Katie Morag worked hardest of them all, and she made sure that
the Big Boy Cousins didn't skive.

"Last chore!" called a smiling Grannie Island.
"Bring over some of the potatoes, the peats
and the driftwood."

Nobody groaned "Gee whilickers" this time.
Grannie Island had made a barbecue.

"This is what I would call a hard-earned feast," said Grannie Island, dishing out mounds of fried tatties and beans.

"Tomorrow –" she continued – "*after* the chores, we'll go fishing and see what we can catch for another feast."

"*Not* chickenellies!" giggled Katie Morag.

And when it came to toasting the marshmallows,
Katie Morag made sure Grannie Island got the biggest one.
That was fair, wasn't it?

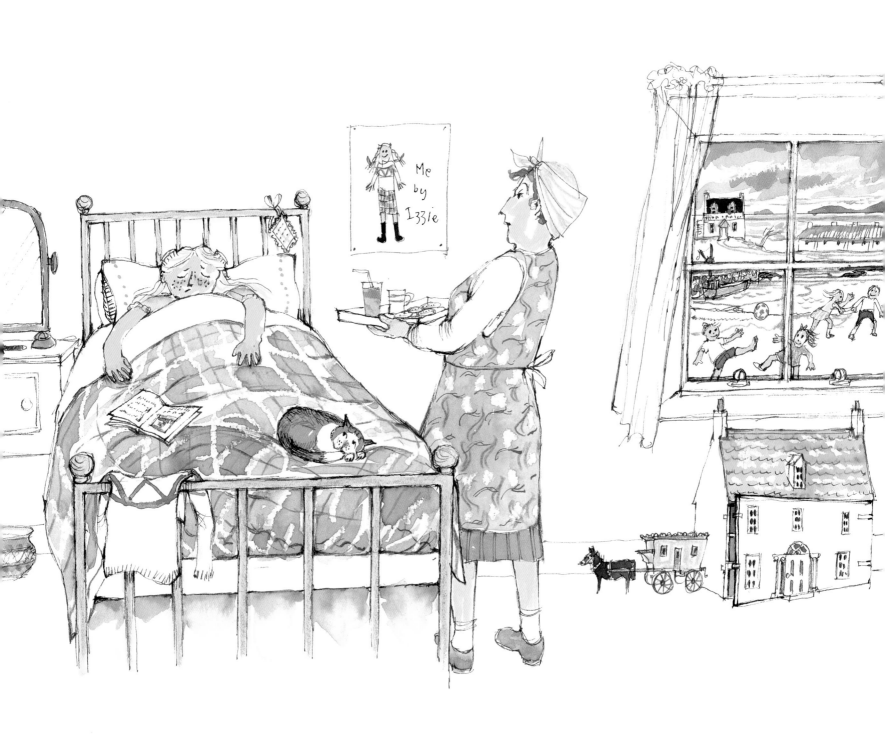

Little Izzy

A folk tale told at Grannie Island's Ceilidh by Granma Mainland

This is a story about a wee girl called Gertrude Isobel Tilsley, who was born on the Island of Struay. Back in those days, folk knew her as Little Izzy, though it's been a good few years since anybody called her that. Nowadays, she's better known by another name: Grannie Island!

Izzy loved going to school, but she loved the summer holidays even more. The days seemed to go on for ever and Izzy would be out from morning till night, playing with the other children. Then one day disaster struck! The summer holidays had just begun, and little Izzy was looking forward to all the fun she was going to have, when all of a sudden she fell ill, and her face broke out in bright red spots!

Mrs Tilsley called the doctor and he came over from the Mainland right away. He took one look at Izzy, gave her some horrible-tasting medicine, and said that she had to stay in bed for the next three days. Poor Izzy! She was so bored, but the medicine worked and by the end of the week she was up and about again. But though she felt better, the spots were still there.

Most folk didn't realize it, but Izzy was a shy girl, and sometimes she felt like the odd one out. Usually, when she felt that way, she just gritted her teeth and got on with things, and after a while the feeling would go away. But that was before her face had become covered in bright red spots. Now that it was, she worried that the others might tease her, so she kept herself hidden away inside the house, wishing those stupid spots would just hurry up and disappear. Now she was bored and miserable.

All they had in Izzy's house was dozens and dozens of books, and most of them weren't even the type of books Izzy liked. Normally, she'd help her mum feed the sheep and cut the peats, and in the evening they'd stroll along the beach collecting firewood and looking in the rock pools. But Izzy didn't even want to do that.

Izzy's mum was beside herself: children need fresh air and exercise, but Izzy point blank refused to leave the house. She just lay in her bed getting paler and paler, and more and more miserable. By the third day, she was even off her food, and this was a child who could eat five porridgies and still have room for dinner! Yet try as she might, Mrs Tilsley couldn't cheer Izzy up.

Then one day Mrs Tilsley came in carrying a mysterious wooden casket, about the size and shape of a shoebox. Izzy was extremely curious, and asked her what it was for.

"Oh, this is a very special box," her mum replied. "In fact, it's a magic box: it contains a secret that will make you feel a whole lot better."

"Well, hurry up and open it!" Izzy said. But it wasn't as easy as that.

You see, the box was locked, and no one knew where the key was. Underneath this magic box, somebody had written a set of directions, and if you followed them, you would find where the key was hidden. Best of all, the directions pointed away from the village, so if Izzy went looking, there wasn't much chance of her bumping into any of the other children.

By now, the wee girl was desperate to feel better. So she got out of bed, put on her Wellingtons, slipped the box under her arm, and set off to find the key.

The directions sent Izzy on a long, long walk, all the way over to the Hermit's Hut, along the Boorachy Bog, then up into the Fossil Cave. When she finally got there, she started searching around, and after a minute or two she found a rickety old wicker basket. Inside the basket there was a large glass bottle, and inside the bottle there was a tiny metal key.

213

Izzy was so happy! But when she slipped the key into the box and opened it, she found that inside, there was another, slightly smaller box and it was locked too! Izzy turned it upside down and discovered that this box had a whole new set of directions written on it. The wee girl was determined to get to the bottom of this mystery so she set off again, right away.

This time, the instructions sent her past the Standing Stones, through the Windy Gap, and all the way up to Sir Robert's Folly, where she found yet another glass bottle, containing yet another key. She opened the second box, and there was a third, even smaller box! Izzy couldn't believe it but there was no way she could give up now. She read the instructions and set off on journey number three.

This time the directions sent her
past the Heron Wood, all the way up
to Spider Gully, along the Seabird
Cliffs until she arrived at the Blue Eye
Lighthouse. When she got there, she
found a third bottle, and a third key!

Izzy opened the lid nervously, peeked inside,
and was overjoyed to discover a roll of paper, tied up with a tiny red ribbon.

She quickly untied it, unrolled the paper, and found a message, written in
very neat handwriting. It said, 'To the finder of the secret: you are invited to
a picnic behind the Blue Eye Lighthouse. Dress casual'. And then she heard
the unmistakable sound of her mum chuckling to herself!

BLUE EYE
LIGHTHOUS
built by
STEVENSON

216

Izzy sprinted round to the other side of the Lighthouse, and found Mrs Tilsley sitting on a big tartan rug, with a spread of delicious-looking sandwiches, and the yummiest cream cakes she had ever seen!

You might think Izzy would've been cross at being tricked like that, but she wasn't. Her mum knew that fresh air and exercise was what Izzy really needed. And this wild-goose chase all around the island had been her way of making sure she got it. The two of them sat and ate until there wasn't a single crumb left, then walked slowly back to the house.

And as Izzy lay in bed that night, tired but happy, she had to admit that her mum had been right. The magic box really had contained the secret that would make her feel better. In fact, she felt so much better that the following morning she went out and played with the other children, until the sun went down. And you know what? They didn't mention her spots once!

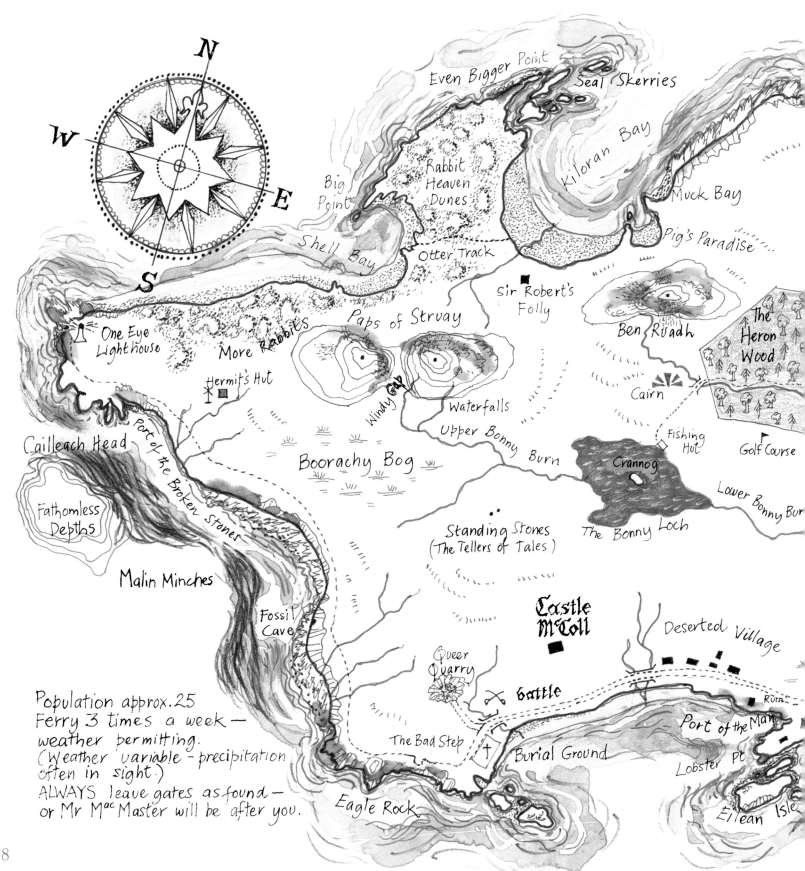

N
W
E
S

Even Bigger Point
Seal Skerries
Kiloran Bay
Muck Bay
Big Point
Rabbit Heaven Dunes
Pig's Paradise
Shell Bay
Otter Track
Sir Robert's Folly
Ben Ruadh
The Heron Wood
One Eye Lighthouse
Paps of Struay
More Rabbits
Cairn
Hermit's Hut
Windy Gap
Waterfalls
Fishing Hut
Golf Course
Port of the Broken Stones
Upper Bonny Burn
Cailleach Head
Booroachy Bog
Crannog
Lower Bonny Burn
Fathomless Depths
The Bonny Loch
Malin Minches
Standing Stones
(The Tellers of Tales)
Fossil Cave
Castle McColl
Deserted Village
Queer Quarry
Ruin
Battle
Port of the Man
The Bad Step
Burial Ground
Lobster Pt

Population approx. 25
Ferry 3 times a week —
weather permitting.
(Weather variable - precipitation
often in sight.)
ALWAYS leave gates as found —
or Mr MᵃᶜMaster will be after you.

Eagle Rock
Eilean Isle

218

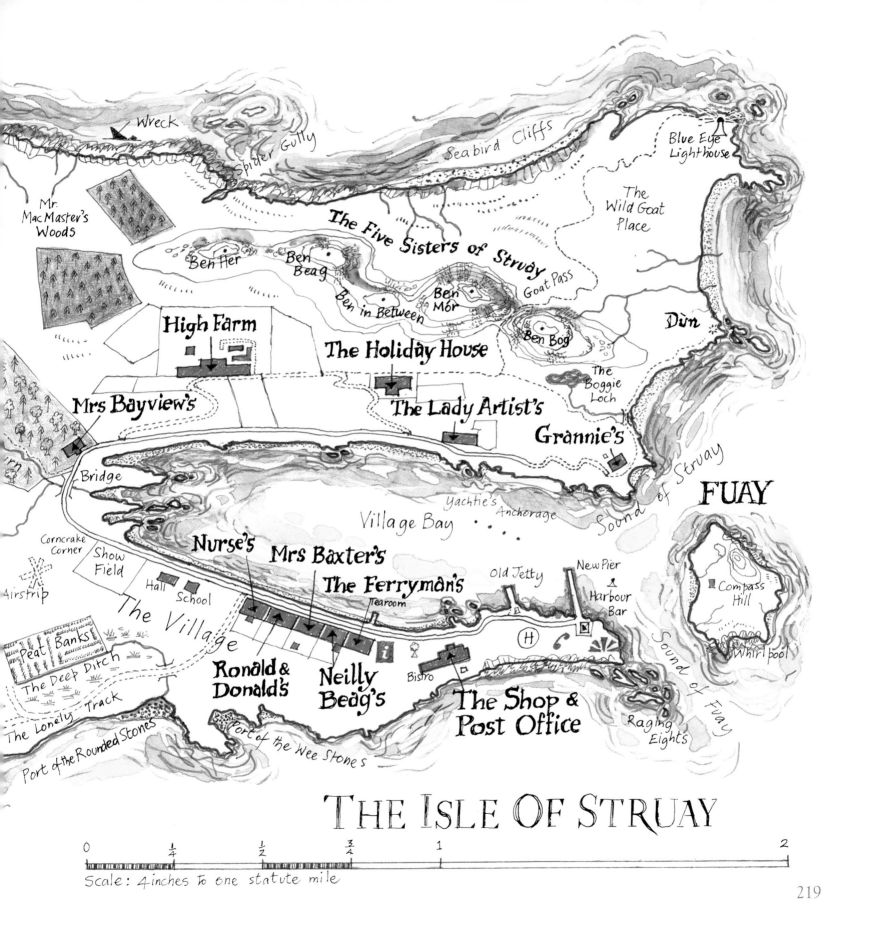

THE ISLE OF STRUAY

Wreck

Spider Gully

Seabird Cliffs

Blue Eye Lighthouse

The Wild Goat Place

Mr. MacMaster's Woods

The Five Sisters of Struay

Ben Her

Ben Beag

Ben in Between

Ben Mór

Goat Pass

Dùn

Ben Bog

High Farm

The Holiday House

The Boggie Loch

Mrs Bayview's

The Lady Artist's

Grannie's

Bridge

FUAY

Village Bay

Yachtie's Anchorage

Sound of Struay

Corncrake Corner

Show Field

Nurse's

Mrs Baxter's

The Ferryman's

Old Jetty

New Pier

Compass Hill

Airstrip

Hall

School

Tearoom

Harbour Bar

The Village

(H)

Sound of Fuay

Peat Banks

i

Whirlpool

The Deep Ditch

Ronald & Donald's

Neilly Beag's

Bistro

The Lonely Track

The Shop & Post Office

Raging Eights

Port of the Rounded Stones

Port of the Wee Stones

0   ¼   ½   ¾   1   2

Scale: 4 inches to one statute mile

219

WINDY WEATHER

The West winds blow to Struay Isle;
Smirring rain and clouds the while.

EAST   WEST

The South winds blow and warm the sea;
'Fine to paddle,' say Liam and me.

The East winds blow and nip our ears;
Liam's freezing, close to tears.

HOME's BEST

The North winds blow and we feel snow.
Time for home; it's off we go.

The Katie Morag Quiz

**Now you've read the stories, see how well you know
Katie Morag and the Isle of Struay!**

1. What is a midden?
   a) A snack made from oats
   b) A mess
   c) A part of Grannie Island's tractor

2. What are the names of Katie Morag's Big Boy Cousins?

3. When Katie Morag delivers the mail, what is in Grannie Island's parcel?

4. What type of animal is Alecina?

5. What is a boorach?
   a) A muddle or mess
   b) A baby
   c) A storm

6. Who lives in the Hermit's Hut?

7. Who does Katie Morag kick into the sea?

8. On which day of the week is Katie Morag's dancing class?

9. What is Chickenelly?
   a) Neilly Beag's prize chicken
   b) A soup
   c) A daring game

10. Can you name Katie Morag's Cats?

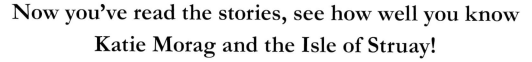

ANSWERS: 1. B – A MESS 2. HECTOR, ARCHIE, JAMIE, DOUGAL AND MURDO IAIN 3. A TRACTOR PART 4. A SHEEP 5. A – A MUDDLE OR MESS 6. THE OLD ONE-EYED TED 7. MATTHEW MCCOLL 8. SATURDAY 9. C – A DARING GAME 10. FABBYDOO & MR MISTAKE

11. What is Katie Morag's favourite dancing class?

12. Where do Little Izzy and her mum have their picnic?

13. What are the names of Katie Morag's little brother and sister?

14. What does Murdo spill over the Holiday Woman?

15. What do the Holiday People get delivered to their house instead of fishing hooks?

16. What's the name of the clan chief that once lived in the Castle McColl?

17. Where is Show Day held?

18. What vehicle does Grannie Island drive?

19. What does Annie Jessie make for the Merboy?

20. What's the name of Katie Morag's dancing teacher?

The Katie Morag Stories:

Katie Morag and the Big Boy Cousins

Katie Morag and the Birthdays

Katie Morag and the Dancing Class

Kate Morag Delivers the Mail

Katie Morag and the Grand Concert

Katie Morag and the New Pier

Katie Morag and the Riddles

Katie Morag and the Tiresome Ted

Katie Morag and the Two Grandmothers

Katie Morag and the Wedding

Katie Morag's Island Stories

More Katie Morag's Island Stories

The Big Katie Morag Storybook

The Second Katie Morag Storybook

Katie Morag Of Course

THE KATIE MORAG TREASURY
A BODLEY HEAD BOOK 978 1 782 30048 9

Published in Great Britain by The Bodley Head, an imprint of Random House Children's Publishers UK
A Random House Group Company

This edition published 2014

1 3 5 7 9 10 8 6 4 2

All seven titles first published by The Bodley Head
KATIE MORAG DELIVERS THE MAIL © Mairi Hedderwick, 1984
KATIE MORAG AND THE TWO GRANDMOTHERS © Mairi Hedderwick, 1985
KATIE MORAG AND THE TIRESOME TED © Mairi Hedderwick, 1986
"Katie Morag's Room", "Footprints on the Beach", "The Hermit's Hut" and "Castle McColl"
first published in THE SECOND KATIE MORAG STORYBOOK © Mairi Hedderwick, 1998
KATIE MORAG AND THE DANCING CLASS © Mairi Hedderwick, 2007
KATIE MORAG AND THE BIG BOY COUSINS © Mairi Hedderwick, 1987
"Windy Weather" first published in THE BIG KATIE MORAG STORYBOOK © Mairi Hedderwick, 1996

Grannie Island's Ceilidh folk tales copyright © Move On Up/Struay Pictures, 2013
Hugh Handy and Annie Jessie and the Merboy adapted by Mairi Hedderwick
Granpa's Bowl, Stone Soup, The Big Smelly Goat and Little Izzy adapted by Sergio Casci
All Grannie Island Ceilidh stories are adapted from traditional folk tales
Illustrated by Mairi Hedderwick

The right of Mairi Hedderwick to be identified as the author and illustrator of this work has been asserted
in accordance with the Copyright, Designs and Patents Act 1988.

RANDOM HOUSE CHILDREN'S PUBLISHERS UK, 61– 63 Uxbridge Road, London W5 5SA

www.randomhousechildrens.co.uk   www.randomhouse.co.uk

Addresses for companies within The Random House Group Limited can be found at: www.randomhouse.co.uk/offices.htm

THE RANDOM HOUSE GROUP Limited Reg. No. 954009

A CIP catalogue record for this book is available from the British Library.

Printed and bound in China

The Random House Group Limited supports the Forest Stewardship Council® (FSC®), the leading international forest-certification organisation.
Our books carrying the FSC label are printed on FSC®-certified paper. FSC is the only forest-certification scheme supported by the leading
environmental organisations, including Greenpeace. Our paper procurement policy can be found at www.randomhouse.co.uk/environment